vocal inhabitants

vocal *abitants*

a anth

stra region

2025

(ed .)

c rlie cas
joe

The pieces included in this anthology were not chosen for their adherence to thematic parameters, but rather for their individual appeal to the editors. In gathering them together, we ask readers to seek similarity and pattern where there may be none.

I've come to see this collection as being interested in questions of degradation, liminality and companionship. At its heart, I would suggest that it represents an exploration of that which is lost between speaker and receiver, a decay of thought, a fraying of relationships and a desire to generate new, irrational ways of communicating.

This inference of commonality is subjective, personal, pareidolic; I hope that those who read on will discover patterns, networks, synapses and bridges that are nothing like the ones I see, and that you will interpret these pages anew.

Darragh McLoughlin	7
Ian Macartney	11
Erin Honeycutt	21
Galia Admoni	29
Katherine Stansfield	35
Maria Sledmere	43
Julia Biggs	51
Harper Walton	55
Eleanor Colligan	63
James Rodker	67
Flora Neve	73
Madalina Boboc	81
Orla Galbraith	87
Maisie Wills	95
Arthur Allen	103

Darragh McLoughlin

Darragh is a conceptual artist with roots in contemporary circus. His physical practice is centred around different movement practices and research with objects. The body remains a central subject/object within all of his work. Much of his time is spent learning very particular non-functional skills most other people wouldn't think of and/or bother practising. His work appears through a multitude of different formats and can be seen as live performances, performance lectures, video installations and visual art works.

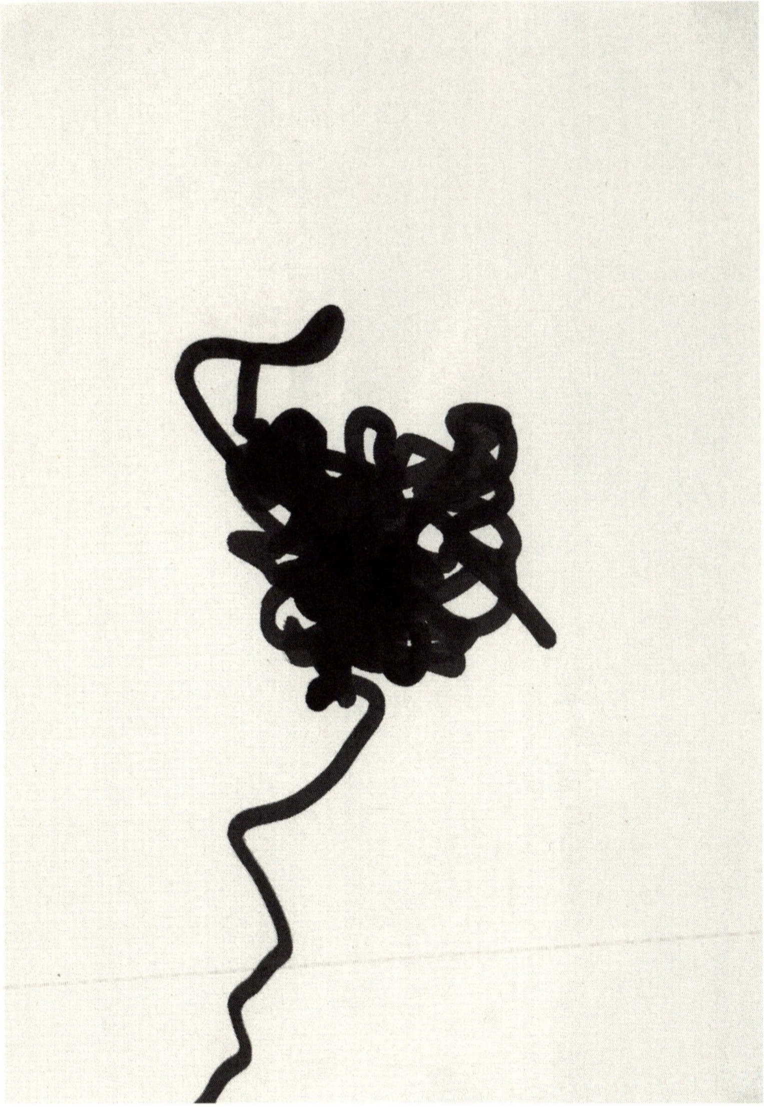

Block of Wood #2

These drawings are created by balancing different objects on my hand while holding a pen to paper. The line that appears on the page is a recording of the path of a movement that happened once, never to be repeated. Trying to repeat a balance drawing is like dropping fifty grains of sand and having them land in the exact same pattern twice.

I hesitate to ascribe meaning to this work, yet, since I consider myself both spectator and creator, I dare to share a few words. As I observe my own response to these drawings, and the response of others, I notice our need to see this work as representative of something. The mind searches for images, symbols, and references but rarely allows the line to be just itself. It is true that each line was drawn by a different object, each with its own history and significance. Yet the line is indifferent. The object that created it was merely a collage of mass, weight, and shape. Symbolism? That's our problem.

Balancing is movement, not stillness. As long as we breathe and our hearts beat, stillness remains unknown to us. Even after our last breath, when all systems shut down, what we are made of drifts away from 'us', falling back into the world. Hurtling through the cosmos, we and all things move together.

Bamboo Shoot

Ian Macartney

Ian Macartney can be found online at ianmacartney.scot, but for how much longer?

The Soft Bridge

, & I would say to him, This is the soft bridge, my favourite part of the body

, & we don't say these things anymore, too meek, embarrassed, broke up years ago but, just business partners but, but there it is, the waist, comma between muscle like the skin was also embarrassed, fumbling its overall question while staying put, vulnerable, open to the love of my tongue

, & we spent our days hunting data

, & data is another word for dragons, of a kind, glowing grey-green to mirror the sky, to patch it, think aquarium glass, complementary to the sheer searing blue

, & it was the height of summer, the two of us, Coil & I, we had taken his cramped campervan to the heights of Assynt

, & data were swarming northward that year, for some reason, so the government commissioned us to investigate, freelancers always outsourced to deal with the rogue beasts, minotaurs or basilisks or selkies

, & it was like a holiday, as well, the kind we used to go on, we leapt at the chance maybe because we missed something from our past, back when we were a relationship, not two then one nor one for one, as it was now

, & they come in different shapes, data – some have dorsal fins, others ridges of emerald, some fish-eyed like a hammerhead shark, others just one eye, pike-esque teeth, crocodile's grin, actually benign though, nibbling only on passing pylons

, & they lay eggs in each transmitting zenith

, & you could tell one had passed by by the coral plated to the iron, oxidised copper colour, lichenous

, & we called it pseudo-opal, Coil leaning on his ladder with scraper in hand, for samples, think bismuth but leaf-green, think malachite deposits on the sway or thump of data's teal tail against the man-made skyline of the twenty-first century Highlands

, & I stared at Coil's arse as he wobbled up there, precarious, leaning against the pylon, casual, checking he would not fall but also so I could feel a rush of desire, rising, the way he moved, just enough

, & the counter clicked to intone how potent the data's broad width was, how far its emerald aura went

, & on the first night we had sex again for the first time since the third time we said we should stop

, & his beard bristled, down there, like brambles, his strong body

, & usually he went for other bears, app buffer   ing against New Newcastle infrastructure, but I was the exception, mouth open, his proud going self in me, like we both forgot how I felt when taken

, & the next morning there was this beach we had to hike

for two hours each way to reach, Sandwood Bay, no roads, a place flocks of data seemed, by Coil's calculations, to be congregating towards

, & they wanted nothing to do with our civilisation after all these decades of cooperation, much to the concern of the government

, & Coil has a permanent limp after falling off a pylon, on day two, sensible bastard until excited, fingertips raising to teach the iridescent plumage of a particularly large data, peacocked purple in the afternoon's stunning light, he was that entranced

, & one of our many arguments, before we broke up, before the workplace silences we grew to call peace, grew from this tendency

, & it was like that game he used to play, Shadow of the Colossus, running on a giant made of stone made of pixels, the strange melancholy in this form of mountaintop then grassland then hill, plunging a mystical sword into some ancient head

, & the Soft Bridge is a geographical anomaly, a rift right at this top of Scotland where the data first flew through, all those decades ago

, & it seemed they were returning even though it was at John O'Groats, that rift, not here, this was not the place of crossing between their world plus ours, this beach

, & last night, after the sex, we pushed our awkwardness aside by watching Portrait of a Lady on Fire, a very old film

, & one veiled gaze fell away while sitting by a beach beset by the breeze, this the cue for the other to also gaze, this little pantomime we do, but as a trick

, & on the beach the next day I try to hold Coil's gaze when he looks me over until he grins or makes a face, eyes bulging etcetera, wherein I laugh, which usually breaks it

, & Scotland is more abandoned than before, what with the overgrowth, the emergence of magical creatures into the wrecking light

, & on arrival, after approval from the Black Watch guardsman, all kilt & laser sabre by the roadside, far higher than sea level at this point, we saw a centaur sprinting with its herd of glowing deer

, & then, after, Coil had taken me by the scruff of my shirt the way I like, behind a dune, taking his top off in one fluid motion like waves receding, the flicker of a film, the wave of data's tail, that's it, him, his gorgeous strength, exposed with unbuttoning hands, tongue electric on every constant of my skin, laying in wait, ready to receive, again, again, O again

, & rumour has it along this strait is where one finds the hedgehog made of grass & flowers, Shaymin, the mythical animal I joke often to Coil is his spirit animal

, & he reminds me that the national animal of our nation, this country abandoned to the impossible beings, is the unicorn, never to be found despite what the Soft Bridge has gifted humanity

, & we are all beheld to fictional animals, was Coil's point

, & then, after, we hold hands, then stop, an inner kind of shame, maybe not even a feeling that strong, just something unsettled

, & we reach the sea, glistening silver upon silver but also pools bright in the sunlight

, & we swim & resist sex, again, somehow succeeding this time

, & I feel Coil watching me as I towel, the way his lip pouts, suddenly serious

, & I glance back once to see his breath held

, & nothing turns me on more than watching one lose their sense of language, become even more their body

, & I think of the one who took my virginity, a banker on a business trip, five years above my just-eighteen, he was awkward about this but I was ready, keen to have this gulf between us

, & he stroked my own soft bridge after, that comma of the waist, whispering, in awe, You are so blonde

, & this was my first realisation of the soft bridge

, & I did not mention these past trysts when I was Coil's boyfriend, he would grow jealous, scorched by an illogical sense of inadequacy

, & usually these recollections, he in the city centre, me sliding into backseats, these turn us on enough in our separate flats, New Newcastle & Greater Manchester, east to west connected as we touch ourselves

, & then one of us sends an image or a video until the communal gasp

, & what a thing, to be seen, to see what he could offer

, & We actually have work to do, Coil snaps, performatively stern, now dressed, setting up the requisite technology, we are still at Sandwood Bay

, & I look at him for the longest time this entire trip, metres away, as he frowns at a screen

, & then he looks up

, & I look up

, & somehow in our desire we missed data upon data, swimming in the air, hundreds circling a point we could not quite see

, & the data continued to murmurate, marking flow itself, what will bewilder experts for centuries, out above this shimmering coast & its northern ocean

, & it was &,

which, maybe, was enough.

Bramble

Erin Honeycutt

Erin Honeycutt is a writer based in Berlin. They run the publishing project Cutt Press.

Tweets from Amber[1]

[1] Descriptions of images from the visual anthology of women and electricity, AMBER (Rhombus Press, 2020) by Robin Watkins and Nina Cannell.

The tulip, Fallopian, covers the nodes with its hood, dolloping lightly in suspension, little legs, fuzzy, a shaded bonnet cap. The mood is also the study of the early psychology of a state intimate with primeval natural science. Desire generated by a pattern of behavior.

She has arrived in full color, bejeweled with a tax ID number and driving license, wet hair look from a bottle, an alignment at a time near its first stirrings. Baby blue matching set to carry the glance backwards at us, an expressive palindrome to get us out of a certain mess.

Salome is in the middle of her set, catching a breath by bending backward, rolling onto the pedestal, the veils are globes of light descending without gravity, muscles engaged. Alice wearing her sexiest gown at the other end of town, talking to the Victorian mirror.

The conduit is in the shape of a ring, a pinky ring, a married ring finger. Forget about emancipation in the Imperium Romanum. Dream materials light up the vanity mirror in the dressing room behind the stage. Designing light, far more remote than a magic square.

The intern sat at her desk looking for stock images of "embracing ideas" like a wave gone over her head. The Google image stock photo revealed a woman levitating a light bulb aglow without being attached to a socket, her red ankle-length shirt marking the cryptogram.

The embryonic hymn of human ideas is carried forth by Helios on a laurel leaf, crescent moon and shards of lightning spinning the wheel of time, the wheel of industry, the telling of three or more recurrent periods of time, an early harnessed power of elaboration.

Like the daughter of Herodias, she danced with arms floating in the air, a striptease of light, tossing in an Old World vice, gathering the light for the great descent featured at the World's fair and invented by Oscar Wilde. The veil is a light beam, revealing a jeweled body, wink wink.

A lullaby singing from the iPhone arriving here from all the way back there. Even the little angels are tuned in. Now all heavenly channels can be harnessed by the breast and long curling locks and pale skin from Greek Antiquity. Listen up, cherubs, to an oriental dance number.

We've returned to the parlor scene, the land of no return where, in commemoration, we cannot suffer the labyrinthine filters of translation, even after the way you said good night and turned off the lights have worn away and is beyond recall. The palindrome is everlasting. If you read me horizontally, an optical fiber transmits 76,800 messages at the speed of light. Despite the glare of lanterns, you have not recognized my message among the many limbs removed and boiled for a long time, crystallized bowls, fruits and blood on the tongue.

Your eyes shine. I do not know continents from milky aorta, iliac bones from the mons pubis, lilac from the ribs. In the fingertip pressed against Claude glass, the world is picturesque and a glow, operator nymph with thousands of grains of ruby sand.

The sun is already high above the plateau. You are spread out like your palms turned toward the sun. Hands like stars. Hair like circuit arteries gradually catching fire. Extending in multiples, like the intended use of the recurrent verse as a passage.

We are lying on a cloth of sand while the Atlantic noon stains the world in light. The heat becomes explosive. It was much the same five years ago, twenty years ago, a century passed. Bobbing about in the mists of Venus, suddenly sinking like a sweet fat grape. Venus is green.

Oiling up the atom blast, we fell through time like a forgotten pitted stone. We let all the creatures loose to live on Venus now that we could see her true colors; someone found the light switch flapping with damp wings on a patch of grass. I have found warm caves in the woods.

I swim far out to sea bearing thousands of seaweeds, enveloping me in a black mass. When I emerge from the water, your white body is spread on the surface of the water, your sea murmurs lightning belling around skin. Light seeks the canals of traces of former orifices.

The letters of Mina Harker unravel from her hands, pearls of letters onto the dusk lying low over Marseilles in the Belle Époque. What wouldn't Dodie Bellamy say to speak again, to speak again like rain. The phone rings after midnight with a manuscript instead of a kiss.

Is that you Virginia, Martha, Valentine, Sue? I know the new electric corset is making you feel like a battery-operated lollipop (or is it all in your head?) When it rains, you come inside with a damp parasol and turn the switch on the flowers before fainting.

Flame above and electric below, inverting heaven like a palindrome that can be pared down to the center of the earth, which is found through the gaping mouth of the creature which holds up the light fixture: gargoyle crotch of a sprouting demon; gossip of mercury top left.

As though we did not arrive from the island of Sappho with our heads and tails of violets sticking out of the sky and smells of wet grass and leaf-humus and long shudders of lips sliding over cheeks and the haunches of iliac, of lilac bones. Running in leaps and bounds. In another figure, the leaps and bounds retreat into gesticulation and the tremors and convulsions retreat onto the floor in a fetal position with the hammering of fists in excess of adoration and in excess of transformations in a viscera in succession from the grave.

Cell by cell, I spill like a fountain. Hello, is that you great Aunt? The water falls gently, where moisture is not welcome. The medium of storm lightning dials the number slowly and waits. When you place your fingertips against my closed eyes, I see them frenzied.

You run under no current. The ridges of the temples and the shoulder blades of the spine enlarge beneath fingers covered with the globules of enlarged cells thousands of times transgressing the enormous quantities of shining leaping all around the globe.

One can hear the sea, hysterical in her everyday life. Is it any surprise that the history of metaphysics is the history of sound, light, and the voice? Good shampoo, Saussure, and a primitive sign language to talk with in the coffee break room.

Common Oat

Galia Admoni

Galia Admoni is the author of Immediately after and then later (Black Cat Press, 2024) and co-author of Art Sundays (Salo Press, 2025) and I get lost everywhere, you know this now (Salo Press, 2024). She has poems in Prototype 6, Objects by Dunlin Press, The Rialto, and others. She was commended in 2023 Primers and placed third in the Briefly Write poetry prize in 2022.

On Sunday 2nd April at the Magdalena Abakanowicz exhibition, I ask Wendy *'If we surveyed a hundred people, how many do you think would say it looks like a vulva?'*

A rendering of the gallery visit is
the underside of a woodlouse

A rendering of the gallery visit is
the underside of a woodlouse / a closed shell

A rendering of the gallery visit is
the underside of a woodlouse / a closed shell / organic masses

A rendering of the gallery visit is
the underside of a woodlouse / a closed shell / organic
masses / throbbing / angry / devoid of activity

A rendering of the gallery visit is
the underside of a woodlouse / a closed shell / organic
masses / throbbing / angry / devoid of activity / mercenary

A rendering of the gallery visit is
the underside of a woodlouse / a closed shell / organic masses
/ throbbing / angry / devoid of activity / mercenary / petrified in all
senses of the word

A rendering of the gallery visit is
the underside of a woodlouse / a closed shell /
organic masses / throbbing / angry / devoid of activity /
mercenary / petrified in all senses of the word / an *unease of formation*

A rendering of the gallery visit is
the underside of a woodlouse / a closed shell /
organic masses / throbbing / angry / devoid of
activity / mercenary / petrified in all senses of
the word / an unease of formation /
imperceptibly unseen

On Saturday 22nd April after the Marguerite Humeau exhibition at White Cube Bermondsey, J___ and I both write about cunts in the coffee shop

Recounting the gallery sequentially is squares / tiles / erased forms from hives of skilled craftspeople.

Everything is body parts even without Wendy. Everything is the crocheted jumper unfinished on my sofa.

Honeycombs dovecote which implies emptiness / which implies the gaps from tiles / the unfinished jumper on my sofa.

J___ looks at mushrooms / their undersides baleen / line up / breathe / crease like open curtains.

I have no time for mushrooms.

Coral is porous / open / round like orgasm (of course) / but empty of wet affection.

I have more time for coral.

A displacement of landscapes / a vulva flowers in one corner as an invitation.

In a few days I will only remember the flavour / ambrosial / and a worshipping of all the empty.

In the gallery Wendy gets upset when I point out a 500 year old violin which has never been played

The gallery is a physical reconstruction of this poem before it's made.

Object I

an empty coffee cup with dregs from the coffee consumed before the gallery visit

Object IIa

a map of the gallery, some pieces circled in red pen

Object IIb

red pen used to circle pieces on the gallery map

Object III

yellow ring at the bottom of the bag replaced with vintage stone ring from the gallery shop

Object IV-VII

Selfies, photographed 2023, printed 2024, courtesy of the artist

Object VIII

laughter, bottled from the second coffee break of the day

Curly Dock #2

Katherine Stansfield

Katherine Stansfield is a multi-genre novelist and poet. Her historical crime series Cornish Mysteries has won the Holyer an Gof Fiction Prize and been shortlisted for the Winston Graham Memorial Prize. The most recent instalment is The Mermaid's Call. She co-writes a fantasy crime trilogy with her partner David Towsey, publishing as D. K. Fields, and has also published two full length poetry collections and a pamphlet with Seren. Katherine is co-editor, with Caroline Oakley, of Cast a Long Shadow: new crime short stories by women writers from Wales, published by Honno. She teaches creative writing for Faber Academy and has been a Royal Literary Fund Fellow. She lives in Cardiff.

It's OK this as far as we got last night It's OK this the plateau / ledge / space to climb on from somehow but I am so so sad so you said you understood my sadness but sad to hear a but so but this morning it's Still OK because we both want to keep going but you feel you're walking on egg-shells you tell me I hear the hens in your voice they want their shells back those birds quick as you like ladies fold them back inside your twitchy flutter their hopeful beaks and better to be sad better to be angry I heard someone say if you don't care enough to shout and be sad then it's already over

Cat Fashion Week

'Banda Aceh, Indonesia. Cats dressed like their owners during the city's cat fashion week.'

The Guardian, 13th August 2023

How do you get a cat to keep sunglasses on?

Do some cats actually want to be models?
How would you know which cats want to be models?
If you are the kind of person who dresses up a cat, do you hope the right kind of cat finds you?
Do you have to believe in fate to take part in Cat Fashion Week?
Or are there fashion week-focused rescue centres, where would-be model cats are housed?

Whose outfit is chosen first, that of the cat or the owner?
Do some people take a more holistic approach and consider the owner's outfit and that of the cat at the same
time?
Are calico cats hard to co-ordinate?
Do people make their own outfits or order them online,

ready-to-wear?
If they make their own, is this frowned upon or commended?
Are there efforts to make cat outfits sustainable and avoid fast fashion?
Is it just a question of what the owners can get onto protesting cat bodies?
Do the owners avoid zips and Velcro because of the risk to fur?
Are buttons and poppers preferred?
Shoelaces are, presumably, a distraction?

Is that an actual Burberry headband on that tabby?
Are the cats in crowns haughtier?
Are costumes chosen to reflect a cat's personality or are they aspirational?
Do these owners feel their cats need goals to work towards?
Has any owner ever dressed up *as* their cat?

How much do cats care about self-image?
Is it true that cats can't see colour, so therefore much of the tonal palette work is wasted?
Do the cats ever pee in their outfits by way of protest?
How long will a cat be a model – more than one season?

Is it noisy backstage?
Do the cats cry?
If the cats do cry, is it because they are generally unhappy with the whole concept of Cat Fashion Week, or that
they don't like their outfit?
Do the cats' owners recognise signs of distress from the cats?
If they do recognise these signs, do they ignore them?
Do the owners open the emails from animal welfare charities?

Are the cats drugged to ensure they don't try to kill their owners whilst being forced into sequined jumpsuits?
Is there an oversight body that tests entrants for banned substances that would help cat compliance?

Would it be possible to use toy cats or stuffed former pets, rather than live cats?
Wouldn't this be kinder?
Would any owners be interested in the diorama potential of a static subject?
Would they need to vote on this kind of change?
Do they have rules about being quorate, abstaining, tabling countermotions?

Are there prizes at Cat Fashion Week?
If there are prizes and these include money, is it enough to offset the costs of the outfits, travel to the fashion
show, overnight accommodation and any subsequent vet bills?

There really must be drugs involved, right?

Who judges Cat Fashion Week?
Is it cats?
What kind of scoring is used and what is valued: synchronicity between cat and owner? Comedy? Creativity?
Or is Cat Fashion Week not a competition at all?
Is it a coming together of a community for celebration and camaraderie in a world that views such activities
sceptically?
Do the owners compliment one another's outfits, share tips on sourcing tiny handbags, bangles and scarves?
Do the owners get great joy from Cat Fashion Week or does it only partly fill a void in the owners' lives?
Can it be both?

Can these owners love their cats for just being cats?
For them, is the best cat a clothed cat?
What does this say about them?

Curly Dock

Maria Sledmere

Maria Sledmere's latest books are Cinders (Krupskaya, 2024) and Midsummer Song (Hypercritique) (NoUP, 2024). She is managing editor of SPAM Press and a Lecturer in English & Creative Writing at the University of Strathclyde. With Kevin Leomo, she is one half of Project Somnolence: a portable lab for exploring speculative approaches to sleep across art, literature and daily life.

Orchid Pheromones

“what if we seedkissed
  to fix each other’s toothache”

“waspishly sexting”

“nectar of the lovelorn
gossamer reasoning”

“lest we copulate later”

“my time zone is asap”

Oysters Apparently

this is my first time

reading glitch cabaret of the guy beside me

gonna have to hold your hand
right. over. my.
mouth

sloppy like the California poppy
face close
fusing aftershock
to know safe
like being inside a song
sugar ice cathedral the most
solace golden boning

arrangement of life around it
having stolen these
hourly rate
singalongs

accruing bright hardness

here for us

Sophia says twirl for the camera
you sumptuous penny loafing lovers!

we got so far as paradise but
while sold out in Pasadena, was free
in Bolinas

I wore a white dress to its christening

desultory affogato

counting

at night the status

exhale of

house world lonely

lucky to know you

teleport logical rose garden

with this sequence you set years ago

what did it wish for, a hummingbird pause
of sexual camouflage

stuck forever in LAX car loop

okay,
soft feel of the back of your hair
the way you say sweetheart
with feline loyalty, okay
smelling the nameless flowers
wearing your tracksuit top to be with you
striped time
kissing stopped lights
opening on top so much
it hurt so good

and hard
harp playing a thigh gap
from behind
tenderness
pronounced tinnitus
so I have to gasp twice
at the ponytail velocity
of how you pull my hair
your eyes changing colour just slightly
as the light does, and you let me look at them
arching my back in the cheap apartment
deeper and deeper
into blue green counting the hours we have left
the way you say girl so my blood stirs
seeing the cat lick my skin like
I was a creature making you happy
and she liked that
pale teal
heart garnering opacity
hallucinates

rough-hued and musical
poem growing a rose in me

two yesterdays
dreaming nude melodies
scared to blood disappear before
my eyes roll back to the ceiling

it's all ocean, baby

Grandfather's Walking Stick

Julia Biggs

Julia Biggs is a poet, writer and freelance art historian. She lives in Cambridge, UK. Her work has appeared or is forthcoming in Ink Sweat & Tears, Black Bough Poetry, Annie Journal, Sídhe Press, Streetcake Magazine, RIC Journal and elsewhere.

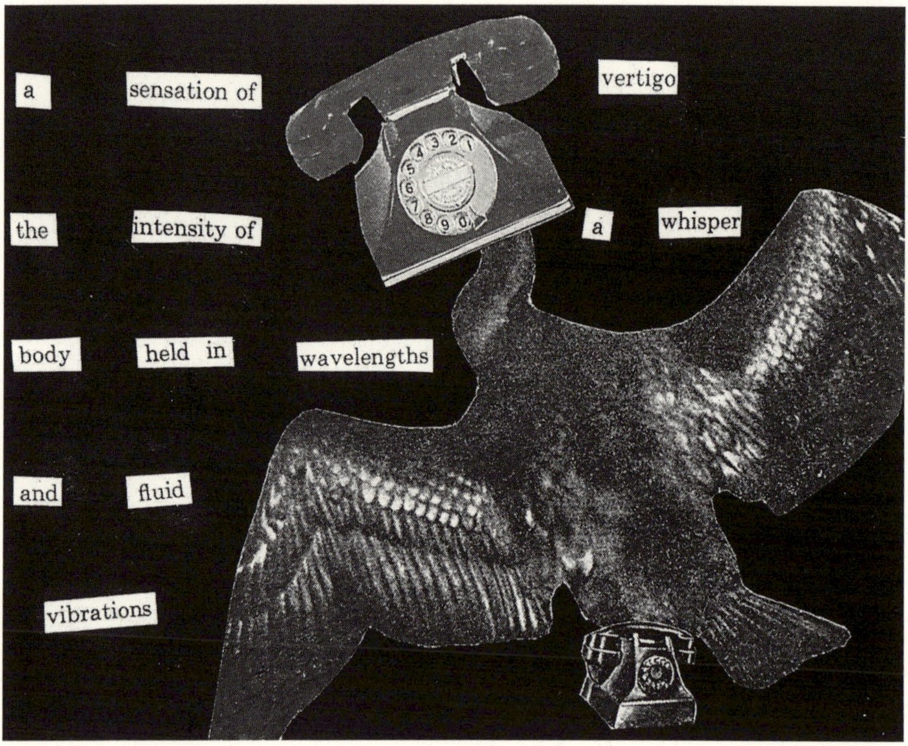
a
sensation of
vertigo
the
intensity of
a
whisper
body
held in
wavelengths
and
fluid
vibrations

Fern

Harper Walton

Harper Walton has been featured by Magma, 1883 Magazine, Whitechapel Gallery, Venice Architecture Biennale and more. They were Highly Commended by the Manchester Cathedral poetry prize and Creative Future writers' awards, achieved Third Place in the Brick Lane Bookshop short story prize, and have won two Young Poets Network challenges.

Cleveland, Ohio, 1986

A man in an orange hi-vis jacket pulls back hard on his rod. A big fish leaps out of Lake Erie, caught on the end of the line. It hits the wooden deck with a sloppy thud.

Walleye, the man thinks, based on its green-gold scales and spiney dorsal fin. *A big'un too, almost thirty inches.*

He yanks the hook from the underside of its gaping mouth, holding its flapping body down. Its glassy, reflective eye stares at him. The man notices some movement, an undulation under its soft white belly. Unsheathing the knife from his ankle belt, the man lines up the incision. He slits the fish from gullet to groin, opening the red gash to reveal the stomach. A breath catches itself in the man's throat. There, wriggling inside the walleye's guts, is a smaller fish. Still alive.

By the looks of its silver skin and sheepy head, a freshwater drum. All his friends have different nicknames for this breed. *Thunder pumper, croaker, grunter, bubbler.* And sure enough, as if on cue, it revs up its signature noise. A clean clicking over a deep boom. Mmm kekeke mmm kekeke. The man cradles its small body in his hands, slimy with digestive juices. He chucks the fish back into Lake Erie.

Be free, little buddy, have another chance at life. He looks around for a payphone.

Suzie, you won't believe what I just saw, he wants to say to his sister. But then he remembers she's not even at home. She'll be downtown by now. Plus, he has no time to call. He looks over at his boat, parked in the dock. He can't make his buddy Paul wait any longer. Time to hit the lake again. The morning sky hangs clear and blue above him. He places the gutted walleye in a plastic bucket and heads towards the dinghy. He can't wait for Suzie to cook it for dinner when he gets back. His stomach is already rumbling.

Suzie is staring up at Terminal Tower when the mushroom cloud erupts. It looks like smoke, dust, gas. Like napalm or agent orange from footage of the war that took her father's leg. The enormous mass deteriorates into smaller particles, all floating higher, covering the city's tallest building. Thousands of people are gathered beneath the swell, their screams drowning out all other sound.

No, Suzie realises. *They're not screaming. They're cheering.*

Ever since she was a little girl, Suzie has felt cursed with bad luck, but she never thought her presence would trigger the apocalypse. The closer she gets to the public's smiling faces, the more she relaxes into innocence. Still, her heart is thumping in her chest. The atmosphere in downtown Cleveland has never felt this electric.

'What's going on?' she asks a nearby stranger with plasters on all her fingertips.

'Balloonfest,' she says. 'We just broke the Guinness World Record!'

Suzie gazes up at the darkening sky. She realises the rust-coloured cloud is actually made of balloons.

'How many…'

'1.5 million,' the woman says, beaming proudly. 'I inflated at least a thousand of them myself. It's a charity fundraiser.'

The balloons are quickly dispersing, carried away by the wind. They look like a murmuration of carrion crows, or a biblical plague of locusts.

Suzie hears men talking about how this spectacle will improve Cleveland's reputation, making people finally consider it a *world-class city.* Suzie laughs. She'd settle for losing the epithet the *Mistake on the Lake.*

If the weather stays like this, Suzie self-soothes, *everything will be fine. The balloons will calmly float on over to Canada.*

But she can feel the air cooling. A singular drop of rain lands on the crooked Roman nose she inherited from her alcoholic grandfather.

Oh God, it's happening again. Her father's stump flashes in her mind. *My fault.*

Her best friend on a hospital bed last year in New York, skeleton-thin, flesh covered in dark red lesions, pus-filled sores around his mouth. His gravestone in their shared shithole hometown, Moraine. *My fault.*

Nineteen years ago, her eighteenth birthday, 20,000 feet above Lake Erie. She and seventeen other skydivers in a B-25 bomber from World War II. Almost at Huron. Mistake from air traffic control. Pilot thought they were flying over Ortner Airport. Heavy cloud cover. Everyone jumped. It was only when she broke through the vapour that she realised they were all heading straight for water. They deployed their parachutes. Her friend Claire was screaming at her. WHAT? Suzie shouted, gliding closer. I CAN'T SWIM, Claire was shouting. I CAN'T FUCKING SWIM. But she was already drifting away. Suzie looked around to see her friends taking off their heavy boots and jackets, dropping them to the dark surface of the lake. It loomed closer. Suzie plunged into the freezing water. Ripped off her chute and overalls. Clung to her helmet for buoyancy. Her friends now dots in the distance. Might as well've been seal heads. Her teeth chattered. Body sapped of energy. She came so close to letting go. She wanted to. Then a boat arrived. A sailor, out on the lake for fun. He heaved her drenched body onto his deck, wrapping her in his jacket. Mute in shock. He found one of her friends, Jason, and dragged him out the water. KEEP LOOKING, Jason shouted. It was the first time she'd ever seen him cry. The sailor found another, Tommy, fished him out. He pushed down hard on his chest, held his nostrils and blew in his mouth. Cheeks puffed out like he was inflating something. The first time Suzie ever saw two men kiss. A bit of water spirted out of

Tommy's mouth. But he was already gone. More boats were arriving to join the search, but the other fifteen skydivers had all been pulled under. The final body would be recovered a week later.

All my fault, Suzie thinks, glowering up at the plastic blizzard. She thinks of her brother, out on the lake, and begs a god she no longer believes in for his safety. Over a million balloons drift further into the dark grey sky.

The next day, a coastguard surveys the surface of Lake Erie from the prow of his lifeboat.

'What are we looking for?' his new partner asks.

'They were last seen wearing orange hi-vis jackets,' he replies.

The two coastguards scan the lake. It's covered in thousands of orange balloons.

'What the hell happened here?' his partner asks, having just transferred from Michigan.

The coastguard tells him about the traffic accidents, the damage lawsuits, the airport that had to be shut, the new charity that had to be set up just for the cleaning process, Louise Nowakowski's spooked Arabian horses who injured themselves and each other.

'This is impossible,' his partner says. 'It's like trying to find a...'

'Don't you dare say needle in a haystack.'

Two days later, the coastguard from Michigan answers a call and rushes to the shore. Their orange jackets are gone, so he has to check their faces to see if they match the photo one of their sisters gave. The two siblings smiling in a living room, the guy holding a cake, a balloon with 40 on it next to him. He looks at the photo again, burning his face into his mind. He rolls over one of the corpses on the sand. The coastguard sighs. The face is too wrinkled and grey to identify. *Bloated,* he thinks, *like a balloon filled with too much breath.*

Somewhere under in the volume of Lake Erie, a small freshwater drum swims, neither happy nor sad to be alive, looking for its next meal.

Random Stick

Eleanor Colligan

Eleanor Colligan is a writer from the Midwest currently based in NYC. She is a 2024 Brooklyn Poets Fellow, as well as a reader for ONLY POEMS, Muzzle Magazine, and the Blue Marble Review. You can find more of her work in Beaver's Magazine, Rat's Ass Review, the UNDERGROUND, and forthcoming in Ghost City Press.

I was setting up all the orchids,
righting them as they
peeled themselves open,
puckered petals making
a dance of parting
lips, revealing blood-red aureoles
spattered through with golden
areolas, craving contact,
beckoning, pulsing with
the steady fury of some
unknown organ -
and my heart stayed
lodged in my chest,
red stone that it is.

Thistle

James Rodker

James Rodker is a poet and doctoral researcher in Art History. He is 27 and based in Bristol.

THE RELIQUARY TRANSLATIONS, 39, 36, 41 (CHERRY STONE SONATA)

For Those Of You Who Have Never (And Also Those Who Have)
running like a dozen red deer (into clouds of golden midges) past
the cracked open window of the Apostolic Church, finding ribbons of song.
After its own death / Walking in a spiral towards the house (6°C)
or carried by sparrow chariot into blurry *Silurian Blue.*
the Spanish naval ensign, worn by the San Ildefonso, captured at Trafalgar,
and flung like red curtains from the balconies of the grieving drowned.
red-ground Himalayan thangka (Avalokiteshvara, or The Bodhisattva
of Compassion) embroidered with gold, and covered with clear plastic.
(*Revolving door*) listening to ancestral whispering (*It Never Entered
My Mind*) amidst the Sack of Rome (1527) the tapestries of Raphael
were smuggled in jugs of Frascati along the Tiber, burned
for their golden thread, and left to bleach on the roofs of Tunis.
amidst the vortex of cascading ballrooms and the *still part of the ceiling*
committed to memory the Cross of Hrabanus and the petrified carpentry
of Manhattan in the January dawn. *Ravedeath, 1972.*
As I Was Moving Ahead Occasionally I Saw Brief Glimpses of Beauty
(autotune) and *into thy hands o lord.* (into the deafening aviary)
approaching (humming with sunburn) the last of the city's medieval gates
bending by phone torch along the beach towards the beached
man o' war. (to Warschauer Straße and moonlit rivers of snow)
and sheltered in the Chapel of St. Nicholas of the Sea, and again in St. Mary
of the Mongols. *Bethlehem (Glimpse)* in the rain in the summertime
Psalm (1971) ((((((*(Mexican Helium*) *Koyama looked straight at the sun*)
and in 1864, on the pale orange waters of the Chesapeake) *drank turpentine*
mixed with sugar) the blue ink of his biro, stained on the side of his eyes)
mephedrone) mephedrone) and what else can be named?
when we lived amidst the lilac flowers, falling slow *The City, Full of People*
Canti di guerra, di lavoro e d'amore and Topanga Canyon in a Cadillac
when Rilke was quiet in the Arabic baths and the bullrings of Andalusia
the Chrysanthemums of Mondrian in the blue bitter light of Ash Wednesday
the landscape Morandi (the pink of the sun) the Cortile di Via Fondazza
fractal *Battle Sarcophagus, Canto Ostinato, And All The Spirals Of The World*
Hiroshi Yoshida on the Jungfrau, and the sound of the steam train (increasing)
all six of his horses shot out from beneath him (got one, himself, in the knee)
with octopus braised with the cork (from the stale Graševina)
he stopped at the window of the luthier (in Pamplona) in coarse wind
Young Sick Bacchus (and the eternal debate of the Witan of the leaning forest)
pork knuckle shrouded in cabbage leaves with fragments of salted
ricotta and black cherry jam.

(When the wherryman stumbles, lamplit, reaching for elvers, darkly amassed
under Lambeth Bridge blue lipped impact delay.
washed my hands in rapeseed oil performing medicine
with dead bees and dried marjoram split my palm in the pestle and mortar
oyster and stale porter leeches to bring back the pulse.
floating down to the Dogs to smell shipments of mangoes and cardamom
jaw shivers and starts to convulse
ink plum diagrams of cracked metatarsals and nocturnes in laudanum fumes
with heavy eyelids and hitting my body in waves and from Margate
we sailed to Morocco, in his schooner the colours of June

Rounding the Cape of St. Vincent, 1844, in the presence of a drift whale
muffled a few lines of verse before setting the schooner to windward
and towards what we knew would be worse.
al-Idrisi warned me of ravens, 1415, and switched to a black caravel
With Water Up To Her Knees in the photograph, on the back
she had scratched a farewell heard distant cellos
(and a fleeting sequence of yellows) Veronese's bleached *Lepanto*
in the rhythm of the waves *I am afraid of the life after death.*
and after some months we came across a raft of twisted figures
stuck with harpoons or the Holy Lance or dressed in plastic netting
from Antioch, from Aquitaine, and to avenge the Reconquista
stuttered angelic Polari and coughed up dried puddles of molten piastres
and sank without a closing of the mouth

In the years that followed in the gardens above memory
Roses in the Casement Window (rugs left outside on the stone)
in ColorPlus *As Long as I Can Hold My Breath*
atmospheric substance blindfold behind a chain link fence.
impossible geometries along the riverbank and came across the hanging
marigolds of a Hindu wedding circular breathing
the allspice smoke from the jerk pans *Sun Zither* rippling grass
on the rooftops above Marrakech scraped apricots from sea green
earthenware in the gardens beneath took stock of my loss
my chosen tongue, my gods, and my fruit trees
my brown and lavender rivers the colours of stained glass rivers of gold
windscreen windscreen windscreen bitter sunlight blue and white
and impossible the colours of the Transfiguration pressing my eyes
to the heels of my palm the gardens were lost in my mind)

in the grid one finds a thousand traces of the cruciform (fifteen minutes
in the sun) one finds window panes glowing in the sun. *Orange
Painting* (1955) *But I who want to smoke and make mirages*
microtonal *silver golden waves* (*here comes my butterfly*
(heavy grain and a kept attention) on the Parc del Fòrum (*The Limits
of the Understanding*) the heat on the back of the bus)
the dark grey tides and the deep breaths and the bright blue latex, blurred
world becomes spiral and like wheels and circles about us, and ahead of us,
perhaps drawn through the water, the glimmer of unreachable certainty.
*Let The One Love Tomorrow Who Has Never Loved, And Let The One
Who Has Loved Love Tomorrow.* (the sound above of shutters opening)
circling eddies of meltwater smooth and ruinous (the Mediterranean)
When, after hours of waiting, the tide stretches out beyond the sandbar,
and arrived in numbers, the crows and the herring gulls, dropping mussels
on the rocks to break them. (as the lammergeier of the Pyrenees
(or the quebrantahuesos) split, for the marrow, the bones
of the goat carrion, or dive straight for their unsteady young)
and when the tide returns, and obscuring their spoils, flock back to the city
in circles.

in the grid (like the orange plastic netting over scaffolding (or the floating
hyperbola above the Praia de Matosinhos (neither mists (nor the map
(to God))))) like the bones of the inner ear or the lead between brick walls
Saint Lazarus and his Epistle to the Shades of the Asphodel Meadows
Meng Po on the Naihe Bridge (the pink and the orange and the yellow)
to forget what I had known and known so deeply (the red hinds
of La Pasiega) gathering the scattered and five years of thinking
about her (at night outside white villas) all at once
Berceuse beneath glittering streetlights (tape loops in the middle distance)
a gallon and a half of blackberry wine and benzine for the Jersey dawn
in the late afternoon arrived back in the city and watched from the window
the river. (hot dry air and white curtains) *Few circles,
other lesser circles, but yet circles* (white birds and the white haze moon)
chime and *Chant pyramids* watched the river until it was done
all of it all of it all of it and then, just as softly, none
embracing the birds, stepped out to the morning wharves singing of whisky
leant my head back on corrugated shutters dreaming of sleep
Myself When I Am Real or *Self-Portrait in Three Colors* on Pier 17
beneath the bridge. *Cherries of the night are riper
Than the cherries pluckt at noon:* (suddenly, soon)

Rosemary Sprig

Flora Neve

Flora Neve is a secondary school teacher living in South London. She writes in fits and starts.

Postcard from Queribus

Yesterday we made God's horses carry
More than they could manage. One by one they
Buckled, tripped, landed; I felt Him shudder.
Then, the flies- whirring like small radios.
That's not all. Three soldiers froze returning
Late from winter drinks, their hands still
Round the necks of rabbits they had won,
Grey furs rippling in the wind. A reminder of
Our vanity, you'll say, your hand on the book.
With each new loss our convictions wobble.
Are we loved? Are we enough? I should not ask,
But what do they think of us here at Queribus?
Today, clutching faith like straws, I don't get up;
Let Queribus remain a dream, a sound…

Looking Back

Clearing her throat at evening:
We were born, both, on the wrong side of the bed.
The terrier curls righteously around her leg.
Positions have meant little and yet -
She grasps automatically at its small hanging chin.
We've cared somehow, it must be said…

She moves toward the gawking patient house
And bids the dog advance (which skittishly it does).
Well, some tend to make the waves, but leave behind,
What? The rest, an ebbing dissolve that barely registers
to those on shore. Oh dear. Ignore me.

She walks in unlaced trainers through the latched door
leaving just the unheard chalk hills crumbling inward roar.

Grief

(i)

His renowned eyebrows
transformed the office: little
tree-storms of energy.

(ii)

Once he said grandly
This modern nation -
an old beetle still running
between kitchen pipes.

(iii)

His words could be like
The sea wind when it pivots,
Doubts and then delivers
The collapse of spring.

(iv)

Evening at Holborn,
Wading through dusk: my father!
Thought alive again.

The National Gallery

My father was a big man. When I cross paths with people in the neighbourhood, they still itch for a conversation, even after all these years. Last time it was a window cleaner who stopped me: *Your father*! That's how it always starts.

Letters and cards still come. The woman who moved into father's house delivers them to me by hand; ex-students, nurses, a man he did research with in Colorado. *People love me because I make them cry with laughter, that's all you need to know about me Bun*, was what he used to say. He called me Bun after Flopsy Bunny, that well-behaved rabbit who always tries to stay out of trouble.

One of the last times I saw my father was when I wheeled him around the National Gallery to look at paintings. We crossed Trafalgar Square on one of the windiest days of the year. Eighteen months of chemicals driven through a perforation in his skin, but he was ready to take the world on. Knees tucked up and in, he yelled *let a dying man through,* and then *Blow, winds, and crack your cheeks!* My knuckles whitened where they pressed the handle of the chair; I noticed grey threads of hair dancing across his dry scalp like grass in a storm.

The lift carried us up, and I wondered if it would be dark by the time our afternoon ended, or some stray bits of light still left. He wanted to see the religious paintings first. Whilst he looked up at the cherubim burying their chubby faces in the tumbling cloud, all I could think about was the canvas and the paint itself; I thought about all the work required to stem its decay. Suddenly he said *I used to look like that until they gave me a new arsehole*. The woman beside him walked away. *Bourgeois fucking idiot. Next!* He boomed. *Higher!* Back in the lift, and up we went.

He used to carry gifts to the nurses on the eighth floor at Bart's hospital. I remember the book he gave Agpalo, the male Filipino nurse. It was called *The History of The Filipino People*. Agpalo smiled and thanked him while I looked away. On other occasions he gave scarfs, posh biscuits, once a lipstick. They all got something, whether they wanted it or not. The lipstick was a plum colour and he made me try it on for him before he placed it in Lucia's pocket.

The features of his face changed eventually. His nose became thinner and longer, like someone else's. I stopped sitting opposite him in restaurants.

When we reached the scrawny witches by Goya he let out a sigh. Spindly boned and hungry looking, they were full of malice and glee. *I think I've seen quite enough of your mother for one day!* he roared. It was early for lunch, but he was ready for a drink and we rolled towards the exit.

I sat beside him in the restaurant. As he spoke my attention began to slip. *Where have you gone, you? I'd be better off with the waitress sitting there, at least she'd try to look interested – other people adore your father you know*. When the waitress came over, he was enchanted and she feigned enchantment back. He told her *I am dying*. Later he reached over and pressed his head against her chest, and began to cry. The table cloth was red, and light from the window glinted off the knives. It was spring.

Random Stick #2

Madalina Boboc

Madalina is a writer and text based conceptual artist who lives & loves in Bristol, UK. Her work often sits at the intersection of text and visual art.

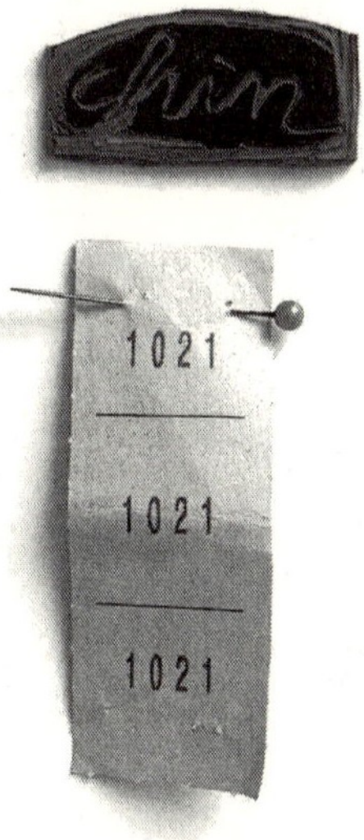
1021
1021
1021

"I AM (S)HE WHOSE LIFE AND SOUL ARE TORMENT"[1]

[1]Sergei Parajanov, *The Colour of Pomegranates*

without you reminding me I went to pick up your shirt from the dry cleaners

you said I needed a ticket even this world needs a system

I go in I say hello they say quickly in a manner I can't quite track

I wonder when was the last time someone did something for me

I say nothing I let their gaze wash over me I enjoy knowing
I can ask them to do something they will want to do

I give them the ticket like I am saying here, this is a language I can speak

I am here for a reason   can you dry clean
                                           my heart

they look back at me, they get it, they have seen it all
before, no amount of work would scare them off
I lay it on the narrow table that separates us
I turn it over I show them as much as I can of the damage

they seem to follow carefully my every move, all the air I
breathe is layered with anticipation

will you take it will you fix it for me

mumbles
looks at the price sheet
struggles to find a fair ask
no price seems to exist
looks up
looks at the time
eyes move left to right
at me
back at it
internal calculations are being made which I appreciate
oh the care

'yes'

eager
almost emotional
warm in places
I stutter and with relief

'please'

I felt a bit like God
I too can have a break

then followed hand finish, speedy service

'take your time'.

Wooden Sword

Orla Galbraith

Orla Galbraith is a writer, artist and musician based in Glasgow. Their work reaches into and beyond the orbits of syntax/sound/interface/landform.

ritual disorder in heathen territory

soil, silt, blood and bracken. blood, bone, bracken and dust. bone, dust, soil and ash. jackdaw, fox, mole and claw. skull sensation, oak and cherry branch. bell heather and bilberry. buzzard and root. grouse feather and final: organic mutilation on open country. a sacrificial lapse of the spine. a body scried for heretical claim. you lay yourself out, convulsing on flat land. you will eat tonight, for the chest is a ceremony, alight at touch. you dissent your wrong-doings and finger your sternum. it is riddled with ticks. there is plenty of time, you are told in an astrological vision, but the sky splits in two: every point on the circle is the center of a universe. infinite points, infinite universe. under your feet, ground stirs. stones murmur disquiet at the origin. lithic limbs like stars flail for constant future. the granite stares back. you return to the pulse of stone, soften in the muscles of hilltop husk. you clamber ganglion to ganglion, quarrying opencast wounds and the circulation of sediment in your blood. wilderness enfleshment, or moontime collision: fistula fauna and your place among the wretched. willowherb and asphodel bloom in your vomit. pennywort and bulbous rush tussock in your fracture shreds. trans-conscious transience in discordic extricable. dysmorphic unearth in elemental aggregate. entity encrusts kin like resistance. kin encrusts resistance like catastrophe. ______________________ -----------------

shell and hair communicate, skin thatches score and scar: iron from hay rake, ploughshare and stone pock. lichen strewn grey across a trembling mound of crotalled rock, more lichen glaring, black-yellow-white. damp and ungiven spot - being scapes and scrapes within and within - itself: a thousand gasping lives grown out on upland scree, a bracken bodied boy overturned and entangled with spirits and twine. you are told, all things are many things, different from themselves. you are told, these are your insides. these are your underlands and churning caverns, winds of lung and rumbling gut. these are your gallbladder burials, bones cracked in calcite, craters and cairns: center points of the circle, humming in the soles of your heathen expanse. you are ritual cache weathering storm. its amniotic purple and you are grinning with teeth. dismembered by hunger for mineral grit, you dig for roots to chew, sacral offerings, and a way to give back. you dig for the pulverized ashes of that baby animal. you are your own/excavation project: every infinite universe, every infinite point. ______________________________------------______

__________________________ ------------------------------__________________________

the moorland unfolds you, limb by larval limb. ancient hysteria wails in minutes, looming ten thousand threads into song. whispers shiver stalk and cilia, scouring the land for news of spring harvest. strangeness braids manifold wheels, wheels of decomposition, wheels pulsating into other entrail ether. intestinal strings cling soot and spiral. yourself inhuman unnameable or newborn calf, dripping yellow vernix smears of hex and hem. the body is a fluid transfixion. is this the homeland you carry inside yourself? an entropic topology of ever-increasing eruption? half-pulsing transition into eco-mental system? queerness atrophies anthropos time until tomorrow. transness atrophies otherness until movement makes beyond, outside, anew. you stretch your arms wide and push against the tunnelling walls of your holobiont chest, cresting breaths of immunity sky. you will not return to what you once were. you are an infidel vibration, an integral expression of mid-chorus collapse: coalescence made cacophony. a green dream with black spit and a rough upbringing. trans entropy at every infinite point. queer entropy in every infinite universe. disorder of the cycle without exception. disorder in the corners of a curious parasite. your torso retracts on inhale and a thick fog envelops the host. soaked through, you drag yourself towards the ochre earth beneath the trees.

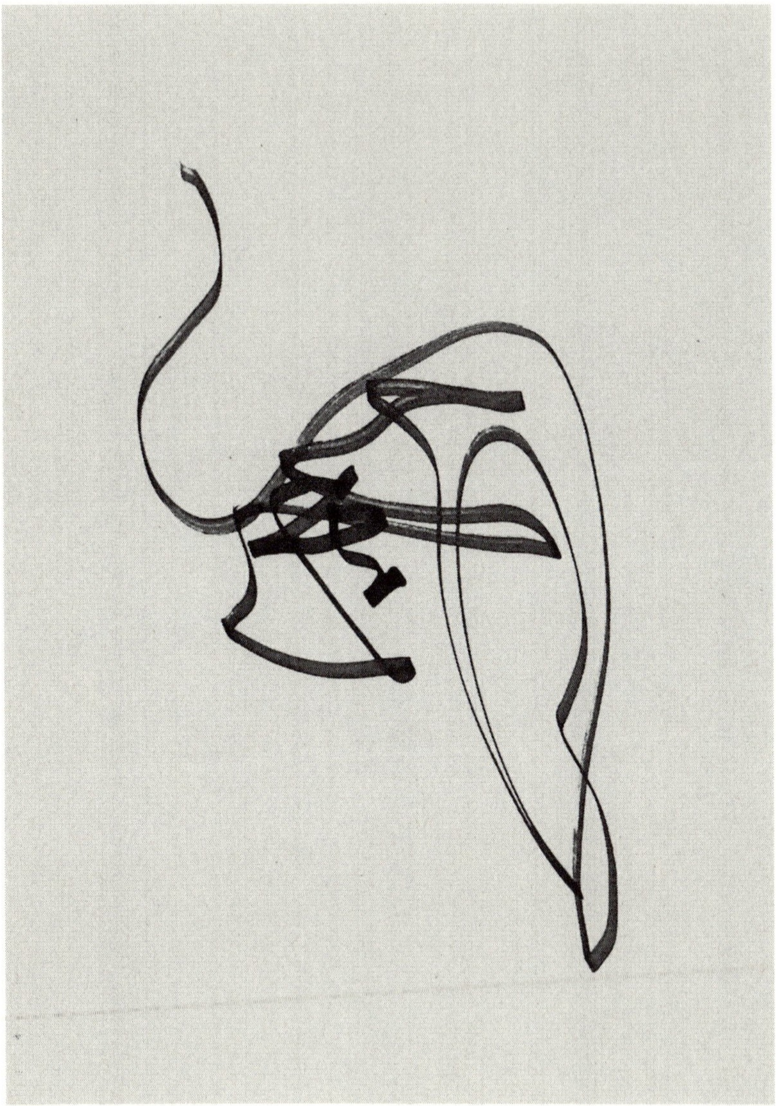

Shillelagh #2

Maisie Wills

Maisie Wills is a writer & artist from Cornwall, based in Glasgow.

Channel 13 Romance

I fell in love with the walls first.

I tasted:

copper/oysters/nectarine/tobacco

Their continuous humming; bright, pulsing, and soft against my ears. I heard their voice amid the walls – unbroken concentration for several minutes allowed me this. Through the droning emerged something sparkling and sharp. Turning the dial, the voice grew until it bit my ears clean off. Blood spilled delicately across the concrete.

*

I was working at one of those new arts venues which had popped up in the city. You probably have seen them in yours. Exposed brickwork, screeching pipes, opaque beers, and bitter coffee. There is sometimes music in the rooms, or life drawing classes, or dances for old people. Small groups meet there to discuss ways to make more of these spaces. I held in one hand a humanities degree and the other hand a year of volunteering at Oxfam. They seemed to like that – this way they could mould me to do whatever the they wanted. Some nights I would pour this disgusting beer, earthy and dark, some nights I would spend hours sweeping confetti off the floor. Then someone new came who picked up those jobs and I was stationed at the doors of the Lab. The Lab was a small square venue where they put on all the decrepit grey haired men bands. It was fine. No one really came. I just had to sit there, clutching a radio which looked like one of the first mobile phones invented. Black and bulky, a long antenna reaching out of the top searching for some kind of signal in the labyrinth.

The radio had twelve active channels, but thirteen numbers on the dial. I wrote them down in my notebook.

1 = Manager

2 = Technicians

3 = Security

4 = Me

5-8 = Bar Staff

8-12 = Only in use during Festival season

13 = Unknown

In the silent corridor before a show I would flick between each one, catching slivers of speech. Back and forth between 1 - *more plastic cups and* - and 2 - *mic seven down haze in three two one* - and then slightly longer on 3 - *ok I'm coming now… from the backdoor… hang on its stuck… sorry about this just hold him as long as you can*

We need the broom in the main hall

Hold the audience for another two

KEG

EMPTY *over*

Latecomers on route *I can't hold them any longer*

Stuck on the latch
the eagle has flown the nest

Hold ... flown ... stuck ... stuck ... empty

I got quite good at moving the dial between each active channel so that single words from each space melded into one another. When I'd drunk too much of the bottom-of-the-keg beer the voices would glitch and stumble across each other, tripping up like babies who haven't learned to walk yet.

Wednesday 24.11.24 approx 4pm

Sweep the [1] coffee [3] beginning 3 2 1 [2] Flatten [1] the house [2] inside [3] make us [2] See [2] as much as you have up there [1] Isolate room [2] thanks mate [3]

I lay down on the stone floor of the bathrooms opposite the corridor. I thought of the time we were in here together. Two bodies in this fading labyrinth. Woodlice crawl up my ankles and the toilet bowl leaks. Can you lie down next to me?

There was an art exhibition in the evening. I was asked to pour sour red wine into people's empty glasses. Shelves around the white painted room lined with alien objects (which I later found out were just made by a 3D printer) all sprayed the same shade of matte black. From the corner of my eye I saw a little girl with plaits tap on one of them. A corner piece broke off and she grinned before looking me right in the eyes. A child's scream ruptured the gallery. Wine sprayed like sea foam - bold on the white wall and invisible on the black objects.

Adam to Tim

Go for Tim

Get a mop will you?

On it. Over.

I went home. I left the radio in the staff room.

Before sleep, I tasted: blood / chicken wings from KFC / Irn Bru / chewing gum

Sunday 15.12.24 approx 11pm

Come in [3] testing [1] testing [2] testing [3] glass [1] glitter [2] tea and a custard cream please [3] go home [1]

Alone in the corridor again. My brief foray into the public domain did not go down too well so they stationed me back here. I'm not complaining.

Another show goes in and I try three new ways to sit on the red velvet chair they have outside the Lab. The crumbling decadence. Where did you used to sit? Beneath a crystal chandelier maybe. Chemically harsh light flickers as I think this. There's a fly trapped inside. Its buzzing sounds like skipping vinyl.

Come

Come in

Tim?[1]

I'm so bored I could die but the sound of Channel 1 induces such a sickening feeling in me that I choose not to respond. He'll live. Crackling jazz music slips from the Lab and my head is dangling off the seat of the chair, legs in the air.

And then I hear it.

Under the rushing waterfall [?]

And then it stutters back to

Tim? Seriously man can you just answer? [1]

Sliding off the chair / slug in motion, I picked up the radio to see who had intercepted the call. I dial through every channel. Met with silence around every corner.

Thursday 19.12.24 approx 1am

Cracked [2] blown [3] have you seen that film where they're all stuck on a train? [3] syrup [1] spilled [1] smoke [2] pull the wishbone [?]

A voice I did not recognise amidst the grey and dreary tones. Met again with static as I turn between the dials. Festival season is not for another eight months - who else is here?

I lie on the floor and think about you again. It's becoming a habit and I hate that. Your voice is like a crack of glass stuck between my toes. I heard once about someone treading on a piece of coral on a sandy beachy and it lodged its way into the sole of their foot. New skin grew over the piece of coral and it was preserved in their foot like a wasp in amber.

Rolled over, pressed up against the wall. My ear flat on its concrete surface. And I hear something

Distant rumbling - a train approaching. Softer than that. I'm not scared exactly but I am cautious.

It tasted like apricots

Beneath the water

Bend your fingers backwards [?]

And the humming returned. I could swear that voice came from the radio. I pressed my ear harder and harder against the white wall, until the wax rubbed off and my earlobe turned red. The humming never stopped but the voice had slunk away.

Mark brings me a mis-poured pint (I kind of like Mark - he's new and always brings me the spare drinks but I see these patches of eczema under his fingernails and I feel bad but it just makes me think of tree bark and sandpaper until I want to vomit). Mark disappears and I down the cloudy drink. Listen closely this time.

I lock the door to the Lab and the door to the corridor. I close my eyes / position myself on the chair so that I can have one ear to the wall and hold the radio to the other.

A droning sound starts.

And then the radio glitches

I'll be there in a few- [2]

Black coffee please Mark- [3]

...

...

I wait until the ones I know fade away.

...

When it glitches it shimmers

The tail reaches deeper and deeper

It's the ocean next

In the graveyard he yawns

Between each strange line the humming grew louder and louder. Until I can no longer tell what is coming from the walls and what is coming from the radio.

Water pooled in my ears
/ flooding me
/ and the world was dark.

...

Loud and angry banging -

For fuck sake Tim [1]

The show had finished and the doors were still locked. Hours had passed.

Don't worry Adam I've got the master key [2]

A crumpled body slumped on the chair; part of me was no longer there. Hands to my ears covered in red sticky blood. I licked it: copper, honeysuckle, plum.

*

I did not hear the voice for a long time. I stopped working at that place. Of course they fired me. That night my ears bled all the way home and the humming never went away.

Sometimes I find bits of concrete dust in my ears after a shower.

I also took the radio that night. I've tried getting through to the voice again but as I turn the dials (the static of each one varies slightly) I just think of you as you dropped delicately down the waterfall.

Tuesday 23.01.25 approx 7am

Whisper to the fox

Before you wake take a sip

Do not be afraid

It's been silent for years. I think that maybe it is scared of opening its mouth again. The last thing I recorded:

And follow

Buttplug

Arthur Allen

Arthur Allen is an award-winning poet and translator from Cheshire.

Ratlets
or 13 Views of the Killing of the Rats

[1]
In the basement, resting the barrel
on an ironing board, I drew a horned man
in purple crayon, shot it between the eyes,
then went upstairs and killed the rat.

The trees made note of this:
that many beasts feasted in the garden
where they all eat – in safety,
with their hands – in the same way

but only one
warm-blooded thing
was killed that morning.

[2]
The sight was in its centre
so I may have closed my eyes
in the final moment
of drawing in the trigger.

The safety caught:
a small white circle
signifying, momentarily,

I pushed it home,
like bolting a back door,
and shot. It screamed,
it ran. I did not see

where it ceased to move
among dense lilac leaves
that hummed with foul power,
like wild garlic in woodland.

[3]

The purpose
that had borne me
into the final moment

left
when I leapt ashore
from the good ship Lethality,
me its fatal figurehead.

Came to the body this way: as though
I had been following the traces of a beast
that had turned on its traces and, facing me,
was filling up the tunnel I crept down,
equal in breadth and height to my fear.

Half-saw and half-created
a soul-shaped rodent
rising without loyalty
from the body into verdure,
reproachful, unreproachful.

Felt triumphant
revulsion only.

Worse only had it lived on,
impenetrably trembling
and uttering the doglike
whimper of chipmunks
who have been betrayed.

[4]
My father-in-law asked,
"Are those your gardening gloves?"
"My executioner's gloves", I said.

[5]
Approach the body like a deer
I have lost the right to shoot.
The boughs scrutinise me as
I bend over the foot-sized body.

I had shot quicker than thinking,
but when I picked it up
by the waist, I thought:
'I have killed him,'
and it made me want to cry.

[6]
A grip relaxes on the garden:
the ferns begin again to show
their tender faces; each
needle and leaf-vein brims.
A chipmunk finds my hand.

My father-in-law
smiles over his frontier,
now unburdened
of the biblical fear – pestilent mammals –
that drove him to Canadian Tire
in search of the junior-sized air-rifle
I am clutching.

[7]

I hold it in pretence of knowingness,
wishing secretly it were made of wood:
flintlock, ramrod and black powder,
but the stock and barrel are matte black plastic,
synthetic and skeletonized in 'tactical-style'
like a part from a child's toy Batmobile.

The chassis is compact, designed
specifically for 11-15-year-olds.
The calibre is .177, it shoots
at 495 feet per second (five
below the requirement for a licence).
        Ambidextrous
        automatic safety
above and behind the barrel
like a star.

[8]

At the precipice
I must tell myself:
This rat has no wit.
And hold my gun very carefully.†
  My throat
prepares a squawk
like a single pale firework,
dares not release it.

The rat leaps
like a flame; the cloth
of its flank tears
with a snap.

For a moment, it seems to be dancing.
        But it is not dancing.

† Comrade Mao Tsetung's concept, outlined in his *Problems of Strategy in China's Revolutionary War,* says: "Our strategy is 'pit one against ten' and our tactics are 'pit ten against one' - this is one of our fundamental principles for gaining mastery over the enemy."
There is not a single thing in the world which is not a unity of opposites, which is without a dual nature. Strategically you must deride your adversary, whilst tactically taking them seriously. Real tigers are paper tigers at the same time. "This is a Marxist-Leninist theoretical generalisation of great profundity" (*Stories About Not Being Afraid of Ghosts*, 10).

[9]
Threshold of fir trees
quivering with vigilance.
Birds and chipmunks flee,
scramble into the soil, the sky
then wheel about
in blue-dark hollows,
shouting their panic, accusation:
  Was it me? Us?
        Was it one of us?

The grackle turns back
  with a whale's eye,
    small and cold.

The cardinals, no longer dumb,
their voices salmoning, count themselves
over and over in hysteria of survival.

[10]
Went holding the rifle wistfully,
listless limb bereft of purpose,

body
(draped like rag
    across my palm)
a metric weight
    not even an extra-tough
thorn-resistant Marigold
    could disguise.

[11]
Over McCafé at the drive-thru,
I told Pat all about it, with a woundedness
appropriate to the hunter who kills.

Three crows come to see Pat regularly
and he feeds them mice on a bloody stone;
his father keeps a crossbow in the bathroom;
I knew he'd understand. He said,

“Eric McLuhan terms rage the soft
belly of male boredom,”

said he would offer the rats to the crows
and the crows would eat them cheerfully.

[12]
(Later, the two bodies
side by side like duellists
under the weight of the day.
I stand by them.
The racoons steer clear.

Do not leave me all alone with the dead, **Henri Michaux**
like a soldier at the front who gets no mail.)

[13]
Spotted while on the phone to an uncle.
Hove the rifle by its barrel, hoisted,
hardened shoulder, aimed and fired.
I had thought it only one, but
it bifurcated among the fronds.

Fast action.
Tentative confidence
my veteran hand
might have had
appeared wrong.

Later,
found the intended pellet
rolling loosely on the sunlit rug.

(to know what occurs in the painter’s head,
follow their hand)

It looked like a seed or a flowerhead shaped like a dancer,
its pleated lead skirt and cupola
an impossibly light and fatal bellflower.

From Canadian Tire
I remember:

a heavy pellet in a low-powered airgun
gives a trajectory that arcs like a rainbow.

How it might have
ended: simply
and ideally,
the garden valley
singing a plain Amen.

But afterwards
the whole setting
is enormously empty.

Vocal Inhabitants

Published by Strange Region

1

First edition, first press

First edition published 2025

Printed and bound in the UK by CMP Books Ltd

Edited by Joe Vaughan & Charlie Case
Proofreading by Louise Overy
Cover design by Joe Vaughan
Front cover image Copyright © Joe Vaughan
Back cover image Copyright © Julia Biggs
All image rights remain sole property of those credited

Typeset in Charter by Joe Vaughan

ISBN: 978-1-7397840-3-4

Strange Region
Bristol, UK

strangeregion.com